We finds Me in NYC
A children's book about inclusion

Saadia Woods

We finds Me in NYC

Copyright © 2024 by Saadia Woods

ISBN: 979-8894790640 (sc)
ISBN: 979-8894790657 (e)

The Reading Glass Books
(888) 420-3050
www.readingglassbooks.com
fulfillment@readingglassbooks.com

Graphic designed and written
by Saadia Woods
September 2022
To my amazing daughter
Marley Woods
and to all the children of the world that
know what it feels like to be excluded.
Inclusion is key and WE will prevail.

WHAT IS A

WE

(pronoun)

I in addition to a group that includes me : you and I : you and I and another or others : I and another or others creating a community or family.

Hi! My name is ME and I am a WE.

I am looking for friends and to be
a part of the COMMUNITY.

It's time to start my journey!

Hi!
My name is ME, are you a WE just like ME?

Oh?!
Hello ME, my name is FAMOUS.
No, I am not a WE. Sorry...

I am ONE of US and there is
no space for you or your WE.

Go away ME!!
FAMOUS, is ONE of US!!
Can't you see??

I wonder..
why is it ok to be mean to ME?

Hi!
My name is ME, I am a WE.
I'm looking for friends to play with me.
Are you a WE just like ME?

Oh?! Hello ME.
My name is GEM, I am with THEM.
No, I am not a WE.
Sorry...

Go away ME!!
GEM, and I, are with THEM!!
Why can't you see??

I don't understand... why is it ok to be mean to ME?
Wait! I AM A WE!

Hi!
My name is ME and I am a WE.
I am looking for friends that
care like me.

Hi ME!
My name is ETERNITY.
How does ONE know if
THEY are a WE?

If you love to share and care and be a part of THE COMMUNITY, you are most certainly a WE like ME!
Wow!? That's easy!!
Wait! I AM A WE!

Yes! I AM A WE!
WE can build THE COMMUNITY!
Wait!!
WE ARE A WE!!

Hi! My name is ME and this is ETERNITY. WE ARE A WE! Are you TWO a WE?

Hi!
My name is RUBY
and this is HEATHER. WE ARE A WE!
Can WE be a WE, TOGETHER?

Wait ME! It's FAMOUS and GEM. There is no US, there is no THEM!
WE want to be a part of THE COMMUNITY.

Look everyone! I can see a potential WE. Let's politely ask if they will play with ME.

Hi! WE are a WE.
Would you like to play with ME and
be a part of THE COMMUNITY?

Hi! This is TIGER EYE, and I am AQUAMARINE. WE are on our way to have Breakfast At TIFFANY'S. Let's go ME & WE invite THE COMMUNITY.

WE ARE A WE! I AM a part of THE COMMUNITY.

Yes indeed! WE ARE A WE!
TOGETHER Having
Breakfast At Tiffany's.

Time for HIGH TEA & to meet THE COMMUNITY.

Hi! I'm
MECCA DIAMOND
Hi! I'm
YELLOW
GEMSTONE

Hi! I'm FAMOUS BLUE DIAMOND
Hi! I'm ETERNITY DIAMOND

Hi! I'm RUBY RED
Hi! I'm HEATHER GRAY DIAMOND

Hi! I'm AQUAMARINE GREEN DIAMOND
Hi! I'm TIGEREYE DIAMOND

Hi! I'm
Are you a WE? Color your Diamond next to ME.

Color in THE COMMUNITY it
can even be your FAMILY!

Equality and inclusion is why creating this childrens book is so important to me.

I had so much fun having Breakfast At Tiffany's!
There is no affiliation with any company while creating this book.